## I AM I

The more Jenny thought, the more she reasoned with herself this way: "Captain Tinker wanted me to go to School. He'll be very disappointed in me if I run away. I ought to go back. I *will* go back and I'll just say to Pickles . . . I'll say . . ."

Jenny did not know what she would say to the big, spotted creature, Pickles, who had chased her with his Hook and Ladder, frightened her and made her run away from School.

"I must not let him tease me," Jenny told herself. "I must make Pickles understand that I am I. But how to do it?"

# THE
# SCHOOL
# FOR CATS

### AND

# JENNY'S
# MOONLIGHT
# ADVENTURE

### TWO STORIES WRITTEN
### AND ILLUSTRATED BY
# ESTHER AVERILL

## A BANTAM SKYLARK BOOK®
New York • Toronto • London • Sydney • Auckland

This edition contains the complete text
of the original hardcover editions.
NOT ONE WORD HAS BEEN OMITTED.

RL 3, 005–008

THE SCHOOL FOR CATS AND JENNY'S MOONLIGHT ADVENTURE
*A Bantam Skylark Book / published by arrangement with
Harper & Row, Publishers Inc.*

PRINTING HISTORY
*Published originally in two separate editions*
THE SCHOOL FOR CATS: *Copyright 1947 by Esther Averill.*
*Harper & Row edition published August 1947.*
*Bantam Skylark edition published February 1982.*
JENNY'S MOONLIGHT ADVENTURE: *Copyright 1949 by Esther Averill.*
*Harper & Row edition published March 1949.*
*Bantam Skylark edition published February 1982.*

*Combined Bantam edition / November 1990*

*Skylark Books is a registered trademark of Bantam Books,
a division of Bantam Doubleday Dell Publishing Group, Inc.
Registered in U.S. Patent and Trademark Office and elsewhere.*

ISBN 0-553-15362-5

*Published simultaneously in the United States and Canada*

---

*Bantam Books are published by Bantam Books, a division of Bantam Doubleday
Dell Publishing Group, Inc. Its trademark, consisting of the words "Bantam Books"
and the portrayal of a rooster, is Registered in U.S. Patent and Trademark Office
and in other countries. Marca Registrada. Bantam Books, 666 Fifth Avenue,
New York, New York 10103.*

---

PRINTED IN THE UNITED STATES OF AMERICA

BME      0  9  8  7  6  5  4  3  2  1

# THE SCHOOL
# FOR CATS

This book is for L. J. C.

nce upon a time there was a Boarding School for Cats off in the country, in a white house surrounded by a field of daisies. Cats and kittens, mostly from the towns and cities, went there. Sometimes they went because their masters were obliged to go away from home on trips or business. Sometimes a cat was sent to School to learn good manners.

One of the cats was Pickles. He was a big, spotted cat who lived in the winter in New York City with the firemen in the Engine House. But in the summer, when the streets were hot, the firemen sent Pickles to Boarding School to get the country air and to improve his manners.

The firemen let Pickles take his own Hook and Ladder which they had built for him. And as he was a special Fire Department cat, the Teacher gave him the privilege of having it at School. He loved to drive this Hook and Ladder through the fields of daisies. Best of all, he liked to chase the little cats with it.

One day in June, a little black cat went to School on board the train from New York City. She was supposed to stay at School while her master was away at sea.

Her name was Jenny Linsky and she traveled on the train all by herself, inside a wicker basket. Now and then the Train Conductor spoke to her.

"Cheer up. School can be fun," he said.

Jenny did not believe him. She had never been to any School and she was scared.

The Teacher met Jenny at the country station and drove her down a bumpy road to School. By the time they reached School, Jenny was so frightened that she crawled beneath the parlor sofa. The understanding Teacher let her eat supper there, alone.

After supper, when the pupils trooped

into the parlor for the Evening Lesson in Manners, Jenny watched them from beneath the sofa.

Pickles entered on his Hook and Ladder and after he had parked it carefully behind the radio, the Teacher said, "Now that we are ready, let us sing our little song."

The pupils sang:

> "If you will learn Manners,"
> The dear Teacher said,
> "Then you shall have Catnip
> Before going to bed."
>
> "Oh, give us our Catnip,"
> The kittens insisted.
> "Without any Catnip
> Our Manners get twisted."
>
> "Untwist your best Manners,"
> The kind Teacher said,
> "For you shall have Catnip
> Before going to bed."

"Honk! Honk!" said Pickles when the song was over.

Then the Teacher took a jar of catnip from the parlor shelf.

"Will the cats and kittens form a line?" she said.

They formed a line, beginning with the smallest cat and ending with big Pickles.

The cat in front stood up,

dipped his paw into the jar of catnip, took a pawful of the tasty leaves and stepped aside. The next cat did as the first had done, and so did all the others, each in turn.

"Oh, aren't they clever!" Jenny thought. "I could never learn to do what they are doing."

Afterward, the pupils put their catnip on the floor and sniffed and rolled in it until the clock struck nine and it was bedtime. Then they scampered into the big bedroom and got on their little beds like angels.

These beds had mattresses and pillows, and the posts were made of logs so that the pupils could sharpen their claws before breakfast.

Jenny was carried by the Teacher to a bed which had a bright red scarf on it.

"This is your own bed," the Teacher said

to Jenny. "Sleep well, and in the morning you can get acquainted with your school-mates."

Jenny lay down and tucked her little black nose in the scarf she had worn to School. It was the scarf her dear master, Captain Tinker, had knitted for her with his own hands. It made her very homesick.

After the Teacher went away, one of the cats asked Jenny if she would like to join in a pillow fight. Jenny was too homesick to reply.

Meanwhile the Fire Cat, Pickles, had gone to the closet and taken out his fire truck. He sat down on the driver's seat, honked the horn and cried, "Make way for the Hook and Ladder!"

Then he drove toward Jenny's bed and bumped it. Jenny was so startled that she leaped and landed on the floor. Big Pickles chased her.

A cat called out, "Go easy, Pickles!"

But Pickles drove as fast as he could drive.

And Jenny ran as fast
as she could run.

At last she saw a fireplace and she crawled
beneath a chair to get there. Big Pickles followed her and collided with the chair. It fell
over with a *bang!*

The Teacher had been downstairs, sewing
in the parlor. When she heard the rumpus,

she rushed up to find out what was happening.

She reached the bedroom just in time to see a black hind leg and tail disappearing up the chimney. Pickles was sitting on his Hook and Ladder, looking very innocent. The other cats were lying quietly on their beds. But the Teacher knew exactly what had happened.

She turned to Pickles and said, "Naughty Pickles, you have driven Jenny up the chimney."

There was great excitement in the School next morning. The new pupil, Jenny Linsky, was still up the chimney.

Pickles shouted, "I've got a Hook and Ladder! I can get her down!"

Some laughed at this, but others thought that Pickles had already been too rough with little Jenny.

Everybody thought that Jenny would come down for breakfast. She did not. So after breakfast, when the Teacher shooed the cats outdoors, they climbed the apple trees behind the School and tried to look down the chimney.

Jenny was way up the chimney. She had climbed as far as pos-sible—and as she sat there on a narrow brick, she said stub-bornly to herself, "I won't eat, I won't an-swer anyone. I'll just stay here."

So when the Teacher poked her head up

the chimney and called, "Jenny! Jenny Linsky!"—there was no answer.

And later, when the Teacher called again to Jenny, there was silence in the chimney.

But suddenly there was a sneeze.

A piece of soot had got inside of Jenny's nose and when she sneezed, the brick that she was sitting on broke loose. A heap of soot poured down the chimney, and in the middle of the soot, right on the floor, sat Jenny Linsky.

The Teacher stooped to pick her up. Jenny squirmed, leaped through an open window, and ran down the road as fast as possible. She ran so fast, in fact, that there was not a speck of soot left on her when, toward noon, she reached the Village. Here she found a place of safety on the front pew of an empty church.

Not long afterward, while she was still inside the church, Jenny caught a whiff of School, and then the sound of voices. One voice was the Teacher's; the other, a boy's.

The boy said, "No, I haven't seen a black cat anywhere. What happened? Did they fight?"

"Not exactly," said the Teacher. "It was Jenny's first night at School, at any school. A bigger cat, named Pickles, scared her with his Hook and Ladder. She ran off. I've hunted everywhere and cannot find her."

"Lady," the boy said, "is it true that you teach Reading and Arithmetic to cats?"

"No," replied the Teacher. "Cats use a different kind of knowledge. I only try to teach them Manners and Cooperation, which means courtesy and getting on with one another."

Jenny, by this time, had crawled through an open, stained glass window.

She hurried to the railroad tracks and sniffed the air ... and although New York City was a hundred miles away, she caught its smell.

"Home is the place for me," she said, and turned in that direction.

As she walked alongside the tracks, through fields of daisies, she said, "You can have the daisies. Give *me* the sidewalks of New York."

She rather liked the sound of this. So she repeated it and wished that Pickles might have been near-by to hear her say it.

As she approached the station, a train
came roaring up the tracks. Jenny scrambled

to the station roof, in time to see the train stop right below her. It was the train from New York City, the very train on which she herself had traveled the day before.

On the train steps stood the Train Conductor with two covered baskets in his hand. And when the Teacher hurried to the platform, Jenny held her breath.

The Train Conductor gave the baskets to the Teacher, saying, "Here are two new pupils: Florio and Tiger James. They're quite a lively pair."

"I know them well," replied the Teacher. "They've been to School before. But oh, Conductor! the little black cat that you brought yesterday has run away!"

"Not Captain Tinker's cat!" exclaimed the Train Conductor. "Dear me, the Captain will be very worried."

Then the train, with a warning toot, started up the tracks while Jenny, on the roof, began to feel ashamed of having run away. Besides, the two new cats were the most attractive cats she had ever seen, though she could only see their faces at the windows of the baskets.

One cat was golden-colored and his name was Florio. He seemed so beautiful and kind that Jenny's little heart went pit-a-pat. She would have been glad to follow Florio to the end of the wide, wide world. She hung on every word he said.

He said to his companion, who was a striped cat named Tiger James, "Oh, Tiger, didn't we have fun at School last summer when we chased the Rooster?"

"We sure did," chuckled Tiger James. "And do you remember how we used to swap beds?"

"And all the lovely pillow fights!" laughed Florio.

"And all the pillows that burst!" laughed Tiger James.

"Oh," thought Jenny. "School must be fun when Florio and Tiger James are there."

Then Florio said to Tiger James, "I wonder what new cats will be at School this summer."

"I hope there's some regular fellows," said Tiger James. "I'm looking forward to lots of good times."

At this point, the Teacher put the two gay students into the School car, and as they drove down the country road, poor little Jenny wished with all her heart that she were going with them.

"I'd love to see a pillow fight," she sighed. "I'd love to climb the apple trees and chase the Rooster."

The more she thought, the more she reasoned with herself this way: "Captain Tinker wanted me to go to School. He'll be very disappointed in me if I run away. I ought to go back. I *will* go back and I'll just say to Pickles ... I'll say ..."

Jenny did not know what she would say to the big, spotted creature, Pickles, who had chased her with his Hook and Ladder, frightened her and made her run away from School. He was too big to fight with her paws, but she knew she must do something.

"I must not let him tease me," Jenny told herself. "I must make Pickles understand that I am I. But how to do it? I shall think about it on my way to School."

23

She climbed carefully down the vine behind the station and began to follow the traces of the School car in the dusty road. Probably she would have soon reached School if a motorcycle had not sped up the road.

Jenny thought that somebody was trying to catch her. If she were caught, how could she explain that she belonged at School? It would be better to take no chances.

She leaped from the road and tore across the daisy fields as fast as her black legs would carry her. She did not stop until she reached the forest.

"I'll hide here," she decided.

Jenny had never been
in a forest, but strangely
enough she was not frightened. The odd
smells oozing from the earth and trees de-
lighted her. The farther she went, the more
the forest seemed like something that had
happened to her long ago.

Night was falling, and the cats at School
would soon be on their little beds.

"Won't they be surprised when I get back
and tell them that I've seen a forest," Jenny
thought. "Won't Pickles be surprised! Per-
haps I ought to take some small things with
me—just to show where I've been."

So she went on and on, looking for a wee

flower, a small bird's feather and a pretty
berry when suddenly, ahead of her, she saw
the bushy tail of a tremendous Fox!

Jenny shivered and dashed up a tree. But
the old, wicked Fox had heard her.

"Yap," snarled the Fox. "Yap. Yap."

But when he turned to find her, she had
climbed so high among the leaves and
branches that he could not see her. Nor
could he understand what kind of beast she
was.

This Fox knew all the forest animals. He
could tell them by their smells. But the
smells which drifted through the air from

Jenny's fur were smells he did not know. They were the smells of Boarding School and trains and New York City. The Fox became so muddled that after a while he went scowling to his den.

Then Jenny climbed to earth so quietly that nobody but the birds could hear her. And by running quickly she got safely through the forest. The morning sun was rising as she skipped across the daisy fields. No one saw her as she hurried down the road.

She reached School in time for breakfast with the other pupils. To her joy, her place in the breakfast row was between the two new cats, Florio and Tiger James, whom she had seen when she was hiding at the station.

Down the row was Pickles.

In his own queer way, Pickles was as glad

as anyone to have the little lost cat back. But all that he could think of was to run into the parlor and bring out his Hook and Ladder. When he reached the breakfast room, he paused in the doorway, leaned his elbow on the steering wheel and gazed at Jenny.

"Oh dear," thought Jenny. "He's going to try again to drive me away from School. He's going to make me lose my fun."

But Florio whispered to her, "Show him who you are. We'll help you if you need us."

Tiger James said, "We're your friends."

These two new friends gave Jenny courage and when Pickles honked his horn at her, she bared her claws.

Then Pickles, looking straight at Jenny, shouted, "MAKE WAY FOR THE HOOK AND LADDER!"

Jenny, looking straight at Pickles,

shouted, "MAKE WAY FOR THE BIG-
GEST FIRE ON EARTH!"

She flew at him so madly that you could
see fire spurting from her ears. Big Pickles
ducked and Jenny struck the ladders. The
truck toppled over, with Pickles beneath it.

He crawled out finally and rising slowly to his feet, gazed in admiration at the little black cat who had upset his Hook and Ladder.

After a moment he held out his paw and said to her, "You win."

Never again did Pickles chase Jenny with his Hook and Ladder.

Never again did he tease any little cat. He saved his rough tricks for the cats as big as he was. As for the littler cats, he tried not to tease them but to please them. This was the beginning of his education.

This was also the beginning of one of the happiest summers Jenny ever had. She shared in all the good times of her schoolmates, climbed the apple trees and went on picnics.

On the closing day of School, when the pupils were getting ready to go home,

Pickles, who was returning to the Fire Department, said to Jenny, "Jenny, why don't you visit me some time? You'd like the firemen and I could take you on a real, true Hook and Ladder to a real, true fire."

"Oh, Pickles," Jenny cried, "I'd love to!"

A warm glow filled her heart because she realized that the friendships she had made at School would last forever.

# JENNY'S MOONLIGHT
## ADVENTURE

This book is for Clarisse Bates

On the night of Hallowe'en, the little
black cat, Jenny Linsky, waited in the living
room until the clock struck nine. Then she
walked softly to the window.

Her master, old Captain Tinker, took Jenny's red scarf from its hook and tied it around her neck.

"I know it's Hallowe'en," said the Captain, "and it's a special night for black cats everywhere. So anything may happen."

As he opened the window, he gave her a wink.

Jenny poked her nose out into the night and sniffed delicately. She caught the musty smell of autumn leaves and heard them stir as here and there a cat prowled by.

"The members of the Cat Club are beginning to arrive," she thought to herself. "I must go."

Jenny looked at the Captain with shining yellow eyes that said, "Thank you for tying my scarf and opening the window."

4

And she jumped lightly from the low window into the garden.

Just then the twin cats, Romulus and Remus, climbed over the fence and ran to Jenny.

"Won't we have a high old time tonight," laughed Romulus in great glee.

Jenny looked at the maple tree which stood in a far-off corner of the big garden.

"I wish Mr. President would come, so we could begin."

Remus chuckled, "Mr. President is smoking his cigar."

It was an old, old joke among the members that the President of the Cat Club smoked a cigar in his parlor after supper.

No one knew if this were really true. But everyone knew that at the correct time Mr. President would walk out of his house and take the presidential place on the Club meeting ground beneath the maple tree. He always insisted on being the first to arrive at the tree.

Tonight Madame Butterfly, the beautiful Persian cat, was supposed to entertain the

Cat Club with a Hallowe'en concert on her nose flute. It was a delicate crystal flute which she plugged into her nostrils, and by breathing through it she was able to play sweet music. This evening's concert would consist of scary witch tunes.

"No one will be late tonight," said Romulus. "Everybody wants to hear those scary witch tunes."

"Everybody wants to look for witches, too," said Remus.

Jenny's eyes began to gleam, for after the concert the Club would climb the maple tree and look for witches riding down from the mountains of the moon.

By now practically all the Club members, except Butterfly, were running around bushes and jumping in the piles of leaves.

"Where's Butterfly?" asked Jenny. "Has she climbed down the vine?"

Madame Butterfly, who lived on the second floor of a house across the garden, could only reach the ground by climbing down a wistaria vine that grew by her window. Before she could get to the vine, she had to wait for the window to be opened by her mistress.

"Butterfly's mistress came home very late tonight," Remus explained to Jenny. "But the window is open now."

Suddenly there was a squeak—then a thud. Jenny and the twins dashed to the foot of Butterfly's house. In a pile of autumn leaves lay the silvery cat.

Jenny was too frightened to speak. But Romulus said, "What's the matter, Butterfly? Are you hurt?"

"I don't think so," she answered bravely.

Remus asked, "What happened?"

"I was in a hurry," said Butterfly. "My paw slipped on some of the autumn leaves on my window ledge. I fell all the way."

"Oh!" exclaimed Jenny. "Those terrible leaves are everywhere."

Butterfly tried to raise herself from the pile into which she had fallen.

"My paw! My paw!" she moaned.

And she sank down into the leaves.

At this moment Solomon, the wise cat, ran up, bringing Mr. President.

All the Club gathered around Butterfly as Solomon examined her paw.

"The paw is sprained," he announced. "It must be fixed by a two-legged doctor."

"Very well," said Mr. President. "Let us call Butterfly's mistress."

The Club stepped back from the scene of the accident and cried "Meow" in chorus.

Madame Butterfly's mistress came out of the house, picked her up and carried her gently away.

A moment later a light appeared in Butterfly's room, and Romulus and Remus were
sent up the wistaria vine to report on develop-
ments. Just as the twins reached the window
ledge, the window was shut.

"No visitors are allowed," they called
down to Mr. President.

Mr. President ordered them to stay and
get the best report they could.

They peered through the window pane.

After a time the twins climbed down and said, "The doctor has come. He has given Butterfly a pill and bandaged her paw. He doesn't think the paw is badly hurt. But Butterfly's nose has begun to twitch, and he can't stop the twitching. He doesn't know that she wants her nose flute. She must have lost it when she fell."

The Club searched through the pile of autumn leaves where Butterfly had fallen.

Suddenly Jenny cried, "I've found it!"

Mr. President, in a solemn voice, announced, "The nose flute has been found.

We must deliver it to Madame Butterfly as soon as we can, to comfort her. But we have several problems.

"First of all, the windows and the doors of Madame Butterfly's house are shut on the garden side. So our messenger will have to climb over the fence, run down South Street, turn into Mulligan Street and enter the front of the house through the hole in the cellar.

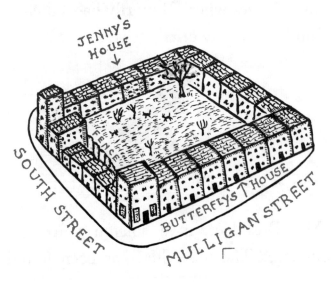

"Our next problem is the dogs of Mulligan Street. They will all be out tonight because it's Hallowe'en. We must choose a speedy messenger who can dash past the dogs."

Jenny shivered.

"Oh, dear!" she thought to herself. "I hope they don't choose me. I'm so afraid of dogs."

Mr. President continued his speech by saying, "Our messenger must also be big and brave so he can fight the dogs if they capture him."

Jenny breathed a sigh of relief.

"That will never be me," she decided. "I'm speedy, but I'm not big and brave."

Then Mr. President said, "Now let us choose our messenger. He must, of course, be able to carry the flute by wearing it in his nose."

SOLOMON

CONCERTINA

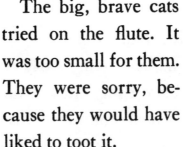

MR. PRESIDENT

The big, brave cats tried on the flute. It was too small for them. They were sorry, because they would have liked to toot it.

MACARONI

SINBAD

So the little, timid cats, including Jenny, tried it on. But it was too big for them.

THE DUKE

ARABELLA & ANTONIO

ROMULUS

JENNY

REMUS

"This flute was made far away in Persia for a Persian nose," said Mr. President. "It does not fit our American noses. How can we deliver it? We cannot carry it in our paws and we have no pockets."

The members looked along their sides and down their hips. Mr. President had told the truth. They had no pockets.

Jenny, however, had a scarf.

"Between this scarf and my neck," she thought, "is a place just big enough to hold the flute. But I'll not tell anyone."

The seconds passed. They seemed like hours, and into Jenny's mind crept memories of times when friends had helped her when she needed help. Deep in her heart she knew that it was now her turn to help a friend in trouble. But visions of the dogs began to haunt her.

She decided, "No, I simply can't."

Jenny looked unhappily at the ground and saw patches of bright moonlight.

"Tonight is Hallowe'en," she suddenly remembered. "I mustn't be a coward when it's Hallowe'en. I mustn't, I *mustn't*."

To her own surprise, she raised her voice and said, "Mr. President, I volunteer."

"What does Jenny volunteer to do?" asked Mr. President.

"I volunteer to deliver the nose flute to Butterfly," replied Jenny. "I'll carry it in my scarf."

Little shrieks of admiration swept through the Club, for everyone knew that Jenny was afraid of dogs.

"Jenny," said Mr. President, "do you realize that you run the risk of being captured by the dogs? What will you do if they capture you?"

"I'll do the very best I can," answered Jenny. "I'll try not to let them steal the nose flute."

"They will ask you why you are running on their street," continued Mr. President. "What will your answer be?"

"I'll tell the dogs a witch was chasing me," said Jenny.

A witch!

The members were silent. Each was thinking, "It's too early in the night for witches. But Jenny is black. Black cats have special powers at Hallowe'en. Maybe her plan will work. Who knows?"

Then Mr. President said, in a voice that was almost fatherly, "Jenny, will you please step forward?"

The little black cat stepped into a patch of moonlight. Mr. President lifted his paw and tucked the flute into her scarf.

"Jenny, the Cat Club wishes you a happy landing," he said. "Try to get back in time to help us look for witches."

"Aye! Aye!" said the members softly.

And they accompanied Jenny to the fence.

"Good luck," they whispered, as she sprang to the top of the fence and dropped from sight.

The Club could hear the pitter patter of her paws as she ran through the alley leading into South Street. The Club heard Jenny turn and enter South Street. After that the patter of her paws mingled with the soft noises of the city.

The Club returned to Madame Butterfly's back yard and waited. Meanwhile, Jenny crept down South Street.

"Oh!" she prayed. "I hope those dogs don't catch me."

Only her master, Captain Tinker, knew why she was afraid of dogs. He had found her in the street when she was a tiny orphan and a dog was chasing her. The Captain had taken her to his home to live.

"That was long ago," thought Jenny. "Long ago and this is now and Butterfly must get her flute."

Jenny kept repeating, "Butterfly must get her flute."

This helped to keep up Jenny's courage. She tried not to think of the dogs of Mulligan Street. She tried not to think of Rob the Robber, who was the leader of their gang. *Butterfly must get her flute.*

As Jenny neared the corner of Mulligan Street, she could smell catnip oozing from the Toy and Catnip Shop. Although the shop was closed, the whiff of catnip cheered her. As she turned the corner, she felt almost safe,

for there was not a dog in sight. Half-way down the block, which looked peaceful in the moonlight, stood the house where Madame Butterfly resided.

Suddenly a bark tore through the night. This bark was answered by another. Jenny fled toward Butterfly's house as fast as her black legs would carry her. Before she reached it, Rob the Robber blocked her path. Another dog rushed from behind. The rest of the gang, which seemed to have risen out of the street, ran on each side of her.

As the dogs surrounded Jenny, Rob the Robber growled, "Halt! We have captured a valuable prize. Let us stop right here and ask her a few questions."

Rob the Robber looked at Jenny.

"Why were you running on Mulligan Street?" he demanded.

Jenny, in a trembling voice, replied, "A
witch was chasing me."

Her heart almost stopped beating during
the silence that followed.

One dog grumbled, "It's too early for
witches."

"Oh!" thought Jenny. "This is the end of

me. Butterfly will never get her flute un-less . . ."

Jenny turned to the moon for help. The moon had never looked so big and clear and powerful. Jenny could see all the mountains and their cliffs and shadows. Her paws tingled with excitement.

"This is Hallowe'en. This is my night. This is my moon," she decided. "I can make anyone believe anything."

She gazed at the dogs with her yellow eyes and said, "The witch has flown back to the sky. Can't you see her riding way up there between the mountains of the moon?"

The dogs stared at the moon.

"We can't see any witch," they muttered.

"But," said Jenny in a mysterious voice, "maybe if you close your eyes and bark three times at the moon . . ."

The dogs closed their eyes and barked
three times. When they opened their eyes
they still could not see a witch. And Jenny
had vanished!

She had squeezed through the hole in
Madame Butterfly's house and was climbing
the stairs. Fortunately the door of Butterfly's
room was open, and the beautiful cat was
alone, lying on a bed all covered with ribbons
and lace.

"Here is your flute," whispered Jenny.
"We thought you might need it."

"My precious flute," smiled Butterfly.
"How I've been longing for it. I was afraid
I had lost it. Now I'm sure I'll get well."

"I wish you were well enough to come with us tonight," said Jenny. "We're going to miss you. Everyone sends love."

"What wonderful friends I have," murmured Butterfly. Then she cocked her ear, looked at Jenny and asked, "Why are the dogs barking at my house?"

"They're barking at me," laughed Jenny. "They captured me and I escaped."

"Oh, Jenny!" exclaimed Butterfly. "Why did you run such a risk? Did you do it just to help a friend?"

"Yes," answered Jenny, shyly.

Madame Butterfly gave a happy flourish with her bandaged paw.

"I'd like to jump right out of bed and dance the Persian mazurka," she declared. "But it's almost time for the witches to ride, and I'm sure the Cat Club is waiting for you.

As my window is closed, you must go to the attic.

"Above the step ladder is a loose shingle which you can push up with your paw. Then you can crawl onto the roof and down the wistaria vine."

Jenny crept to the attic, pushed up the shingle, crawled onto the roof and looked far down into the garden.

At the foot of the vine stood the members of the Cat Club. When they saw Jenny, they began to jump with excitement. She could see Mr. President motioning them to stand still.

"That's just like Mr. President," thought Jenny. "He's afraid my friends will bother me and make me fall. But I'll not fall."

Jenny dug her claws into the trunk of the vine and began to climb down carefully.

As she passed Butterfly's window, she called, "Whoo hoo."

Butterfly tooted her flute.

Jenny continued to climb down until she was within jumping distance of the ground. At this point, she let go the vine and leaped safely into the Club.

"Jenny!" cried the members. "Jenny delivered the flute! Now our friend, Butterfly, will get well."

Then the Cat Club ran to the maple tree, scrambled up into its branches and began

to look for witches riding down from the
mountains of the moon.

# About the Author-Illustrator

ESTHER AVERILL has written over twenty children's books, many of which she has also illustrated. She was founding editor of the Domino Press in 1931 and has worked in the children's section of the New York Public Library. She received the *New York Times* award for illustration in 1954. *The School for Cats* and *Jenny's Moonlight Adventure* are two of the many lovely stories about the shy little cat, Jenny Linsky.

# SKYLARK BOOKS
## can be *your* special friends

☐ 15615 **THE WHITE STALLION** by Elizabeth Shub.
$2.75 ($3.25 in Canada)  Long ago, a proud white
stallion roamed the plains of Texas.  Cowboys said
he was the greatest horse that ever lived.  Gretchen
discovers, in a scary, exciting adventure, that they
were right.

☐ 15777 **JACK GALAXY, SPACE COP**
by Robert Kraus.  $2.75 ($3.25 in Canada)
Jack zooms through the universe fighting space
crime with his best friend Sally and Jojo the space
dog.  Giant hamburgers are taking over the world
and only Jack & his friends can save the day!

☐ 15711 **BUMPS IN THE NIGHT** by Harry Allard.
$2.50 ($2.95 in Canada) Dudley the Stork finds out
his new house is haunted and is determined to find
out just who the ghost is.

Buy them wherever paperback books are sold—or order below.

**Bantam Books, Dept. SK12, 414 East Golf Road, Des Plaines, IL  60016**

Please send me the items I have checked above.  I am enclosing $_____
(please add $2.00 to cover postage and handling).  Send check or money
order, no cash or C.O.D.s please.

Mr/Ms _____

Address _____

City/State _____ Zip _____

SK12-11/90

Please allow four to six weeks for delivery.
Prices and availability subject to change without notice.

## Are you a good detective?
## Solve tricky mysteries with
## ENCYCLOPEDIA BROWN!
# by Donald Sobol

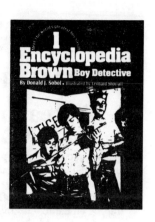

Match wits with the great sleuth in sneakers Leroy (Encyclopedia) Brown! Each Encyclopedia Brown book contains ten baffling cases for you to solve. You'll find mysteries such as "The Case of the Worm Pills" and "The Case of the Masked Robber."

Get ready for fun with the great detective! You'll want to solve each one of these mysteries. Order today!

# BANTAM SKYLARK BOOKS
# A Reading Adventure

*A stranger on earth needs Erik's help!*

☐ **15694 THE FALLEN SPACEMAN Lee Harding     $2.75**
Up above the earth a mysterious spaceship watches. One small
alien, tucked inside a huge spacesuit, is working outside the craft
when it suddenly blasts off. Poor Tyro alone and frightened, is
trapped on Earth. Luckily, it's Erik who finds him first.

### Can there be such a thing as too much chocolate?

☐ **15639 THE CHOCOLATE TOUCH Patrick Skene
Catling $2.95**
John Midas loves chocolate more than anything else in the world.
Until the day he finds a funny coin, trades it for a box of chocolate
and—*the chocolate touch*. Suddenly, everything tastes like
chocolate and John finds out it's possible to get too much of a very
good thing.

### Simon's new best friend is a ghost!

☐ **15622 GHOST IN MY SOUP Judi Miller  $2.75**
Something funny is going on at Scott's house. Someone—or
something—is moving things around, stealing and making all
kinds of trouble which Scott gets blamed for. Only Scott knows
what's *really* going on, and who—or what—is to blame!

- - - - - - - - - - - - - - - - - - - - - - -

**Bantam Books, Dept. SK11, 414 East Golf Road, Des Plaines, IL 60016**

Please send me the items I have checked above. I am enclosing $_____
(please add $2.00 to cover postage and handling). Send check or money
order, no cash or C.O.D.s please.

Mr/Ms _____

Address _____

City/State _____ Zip _____

SK11-11/89

Please allow four to six weeks for delivery.
Prices and availability subject to change without notice.

# Laugh yourself silly!

**?**

What do you get from a nervous cow? Milkshakes.

What's an overgrown vampire? A big pain in the neck.

What did Betsy Ross say when she ripped her flag? "Darn it."

What do you say if you meet a ghost? "How do you boo?"

You'll love all the hilarious riddles in these books—about everything from pets to monsters! They're zany and crazy and screamingly funny—get ready to howl!

**Collect all these riddle books by David A. Adler. Order today!**